The House That Biff Built

by Janet Campbell
Illustrated by Tom Cooke

Featuring Jim Henson's
Sesame Street Muppets

A SESAME STREET/GOLDEN PRESS BOOK
Published by Western Publishing Company, Inc.
in conjunction with Children's Television Workshop.

This is the house that Biff built.

foreman

blueprint

This is the plan

the architect drew

For the house

that Biff built.

dump truck

back hoe

excavation

These are the machines

that dug up the ground

To make the excavation

For the house

that Biff built.

bulldozer

This is the cement mixer

    that poured the cement

To make the foundation

In the excavation

For the house

    that Biff built.

foundation mold

cement mixer

foundation

This is the mason

who laid the bricks

To make the walls

Above the foundation

Of the house

that Biff built.

trowel

bricks

hod carrier

MORTAR

mixing box

tar paper

insulation

TAR

brush

This is the roofer

who rolled out the tar paper

To make the roof

On top of the walls

Above the foundation

Of the house

that Biff built.

scaffolding

saw

plumb
line

carpenter's leve

These are the carpenters

who hammered and sawed

To make the rooms

Of the house

that Biff built.

hammer

nails

These are the electricians

who put in the wires

For the electric lights

To light up the rooms

Of the house

that Biff built.

wire
clippers

wires

stepladder

screwdriver

faucet

pipes

This is the plumber

who put in the pipes

To carry the water

Into the kitchen and bathroom

Of the house

that Biff built.

wrench

blow torch

spackling paste

These are the painters

    who spackled the walls

    and painted them all

To make the rooms pretty

And finish the house

    that Biff built.

paint cans

These are the people

who brought all their things—

Their lamps and beds,

Tables and chairs,

Books and toys,

And teddy bears,

And moved into the house

that Biff built.

moving van

DAVIS
MOVERS

And this is the party

  they had that night

For the architect, the mason,

The carpenters, the electricians,

The plumbers, the painters,

And all of the workers

Who worked so hard

On the house

  that Biff built.